For Maggie Dort.

part one.

overqualified

Dear Irving Oil,

I am writing to apply for a job with your company, and I have included my resume for your review. You will find that every reference and each previous job will check out as valid, but I think that it's important to be honest: my assigned mission is to take you down, from the inside.

Little things, you know? I'm supposed to fudge your tax records a bit, leave you open to audit. Misdirect shipments. Eat away at your profits. I'm here to speed up the peak oil problem, because after that the world starts getting better.

And it gets better and better, Irving. By the time I'm born, a hundred years from now, there's no crime. There's no pollution. Human beings are living to almost two hundred. Every year that number gets bigger. Scientists say my generation might live forever.

I volunteered to be sent into the past. How could any kid grow up in a perfect world, hearing about crime and violence and war and sexually transmitted diseases, and not think, "Fuck, that sounds exciting." My mission is sabotage, but that does neither of us any good. I want to help you. I don't want to live forever, Irving. I want to live fast and die young. That's a thing, right? I want to be injured in a daring rooftop escape.

I spent seventy years sitting around in classrooms, just learning. Oh, how can we live longer? Oh, how can we make ourselves more perfect? Oh, we're all very wise. But I want to kill something. I want to get drunk in a bar and take a pool cue and fuck up a dude with a scar down the side of his face. I want a scar down the side of my own face. I want to get an alcoholic woman pregnant, and when that little freak squirts out, nine months later, I want to tell him, "Live for today, you retarded little shit. The end is near."

Joey Comeau

Dear HBO,

I want a job fighting professional boxers on your cable network. I have no training. I have no resume. I am small but I am nearly invincible, HBO. Ask anyone. My brother Adrian is in the hospital. He got hit by a drunk driver, and our doctor put a hand on my shoulder and said, "We have to stay optimistic." My girlfriend Susan told me, "He's going to pull through," and my mother keeps saying, "A mother should never have to outlive her children." They've been watching too much daytime TV, I think. Everyone dies in daytime TV. In the movies, the hero lives forever. My brother and I have always lived in a buddy-cop movie. Like good cop bad cop, only we're both the bad cop.

Sometimes my phone rings in the middle of the night and it's John Wayne, crying. He's afraid, and he needs me to tell him everything will be okay. There's a beep and I switch over to the other line and it's Bruce Willis and he's heard that I have a good heart. Maybe I can help him get through this rough patch.

Clint Eastwood is at the door, and he's fallen off his bike. Have I got a Band-Aid? I don't have time for this shit, man, because I've got a train to stop. I have to bring down a madman. I have to unmask the president. I have to punch holes in manholes. I have to tear up payphones like they were phone books.

I don't make collect calls, I make the operator pay.

"Motherfucker," I tell him.

Joey Comeau

Dear Xerox Canada,

Thank you for taking the time to consider my resume, even though I don't have one.

MICROSOFT CANADA JOB HISTORY IBM

I have been programming Perl for eight years, on every business-appropriate platform there is, and I've been around long enough to understand that there are no human beings reading this.

PENTIUM APPLE PARAMOUNT STUDIOS GENERAL MOTORS ENGINEERING

You're a room of machines looking for keywords, the same way that my ISP searches for flagged keywords in my emails and lets the authorities know if I talk about certain subjects.

PERL, UNIX, LINUX, WINDOWS, PRIME MINISTER, PONY, MY PET MONSTER, MIKE DOUGHTY, DANCE, DANCE, DRUNK DRIVER, REVOLUTION, COBOL, PASCAL, ART, DECO, ADRIAN

So I could write anything I want, and your warrior robots will kindly index me because I mention HARVARD, because I mention MIT RESEARCH LABS, because I mention the YALE KNITTING CIRCLE. Your lead robot will look over the lists that the lower robots are churning out, and say,

"There are too many, motherfucker! Sort them by year of graduation, and we'll take the youngest into consideration. They'll work for peanuts." All the robots will laugh in that horrific robot voice. And as long as I get the most hits from the search engines, you'll hire me.

GRADUATED IN 2004 GRADUATED WITH HONOURS JENNIFER LOPEZ HOSPITAL TERROR SUSAN GIRLFRIEND $insurance-name $3psn-vb-pst

So, I'll just load up this email up with keywords RELIABLE PERFECTIONIST LIAR LIAR PERL C++ C# C*&%^$^ VISUAL BASIC AUDIO BASIC JAVA BeOS GENTLE-MEN'S SOCIAL and in amongst all the keywords, will your robots find the real message?

I'm coming down there. I have a hammer and I'm going to use it to crack your robots' heads. I'm going to bust open the sides of your machines so that YALE PRINCETON NO CRIMINAL HISTORY BACKGROUND SEXUAL-ITY CHECK RESULTS VOTED WHICH WAY spill out all over your shiny marble floor.

Joey Comeau

Dear Absolut Vodka,

I am writing to apply for a position in your advertising department. I have included my resume, which outlines my extensive experience with marketing campaigns, and with the development of brand initiatives for alcoholic beverages. These materials should give you an adequate overview of my professional experience, so I would like to use this cover letter to tell you a story.

When I was eight, my brother and I used to fight to the death on the roof of the barn. There wasn't much else to do out in the country, with those fields and that one red road. Not red like blood. Red like clay. Red like the desert cliffs in western movies. We rode our bikes on that red pavement. We swam in the warm water. We fought to the death.

It wasn't a tall barn, maybe twelve feet high, with old farm equipment laid against the side, rusted spiked ladders for our small hands. We climbed up and stood on that roof. In our heads this was the climax of an action movie. We'd never seen an action movie that took place above a vineyard, but that was okay. This wasn't a vineyard. It was a lost temple, overgrown in the jungle. We made up characters for ourselves. We hummed our own fight music.

Adrian was always a better fighter. He knew how to make me angry, and being angry made me sloppy. I lunged. I tried to shove him and he spun around, throwing me off balance. I fell off the edge, backwards, Adrian laughing. I hit the ground hard and my lungs went empty. Grass in my mouth, mud between my fingers.

I climbed back up, tearing my hands on rust and too angry to care. Adrian laughed until I was right there, until I was up on that barn again and I almost had him, and then he turned and leapt. He never looked first.

I learned that from my younger brother. You don't look first. You jump and you trust that your body knows what to do. You don't know what I mean, do you, Absolut? Your commercials are all pretty pictures and clever design. They're very attractive. I am applying for a job, because I don't think you understand what it means to be cool or strong or invincible. You of all people should know. That is what alcohol does. It makes you strong. You can fight anyone. You can seduce any woman. You can drive faster than death.

Joey Comeau

Dear Levi Strauss & Co.,

I am writing to apply for a retail position, as advertised on your website. I have managerial experience, and I recognize that I am overqualified for sales, but I want something simple. I want to find sizes for cranky customers. I want to come back late from my lunch break, and I don't want to bring my work home with me. I have my own life. Like tonight.

Tonight at dinner my mother showed me three photographs from when Adrian and I were young. In the first, the three of us are sitting in the cage of a fair ride called "The Spider." My mother has huge punk rock hair. Adrian and I are wearing ugly sweaters and grinning because we won. We fought and fought to be allowed on the ride and finally my mother relented.

In the second picture, the ride is in motion and my mother is holding onto the bar, smiling while our little faces are twisted with confusion and horror. Our grins are gone. This was not what we expected. We made a mistake.

In the final picture, Adrian and I are not visible at all, hiding in her lap, crying. In the picture, my mother is laughing, hard.

Anyway, as long as I come to work and do my job, what do you care?

Joey Comeau

Dear Park Lane Mall,

Hello, I am seeking a position as Santa Claus. I am including my resume, but I ask that you also pay special attention to this cover letter — I hope to show why you should look beyond my lack of experience with children to my other outstanding qualifications.

My resume will indicate that I worked for ten years as the foreman of an assembly line at Mattel. Day after day I over-saw the construction of thousands and thousands of toys for children. My employees were mostly middle-aged men, which didn't sit right with me. I used my considerable sway in the company to influence hiring practices, instituting signing bonuses and additional benefits for people of small stature.

I had new uniforms designed! Green slippers and ridiculous hats. I made everyone sing in time as they worked. This was my workshop full of elves. Everything was perfect.

For a while.

You will notice a period of unemployment on my resume, as I faced several harassment suits and three charges of racism from Irish midgets I allegedly referred to as "my North Pole leprechauns." They charged me with theft, too, when they found my bag of toys hidden away behind the lockers.

When I became unemployed I had nowhere else to go. I got very hungry, very fast, and took to sneaking into people's houses, looking for milk and cookies. That's all I ever took, no matter what the police reports said. Milk and cookies. The Jones family filed a fraudulent insurance claim, and they are no longer on my "nice" list. I found that it was impossible to get in through chimneys, so usually I just busted in a window.

I think that my qualifications speak for themselves, and frankly, I think you'd be lucky to have me as a Santa. What kind of person applies for a job like that, anyway, having little kids sit on their johnson all day? Perverts, man. Perverts. I'm doing this because I have no other choice. It's my calling. I don't even like kids.

Joey Comeau

Dear RAND,

I am writing to apply for a job with the RAND Corporation.
The first time I heard of the RAND Corporation was on
The X-Files, the conspiracy-theory-heavy television show I
was obsessed with in high school. I watched every episode.
That was the beginning of my paranoia, my belief that there
are huge corporations behind everything. That everything
that happens in the world happens for a reason.

This isn't the first letter I've written you, though I don't
know if you remember. When I was just out of high school,
there was a shooting in Colorado. Thirteen dead and
twenty-three wounded. Children killed by other children. I
spent a lot of time sitting in front of the television with the
sound off. I found your address on the Internet, RAND, and
I wrote you the following letter.

"I don't understand about Columbine. Please write back."

I know exactly what it said, RAND, because it came back to
me unopened. I still have it.

Two years later, when two planes full of people flew into the
side of those buildings in New York City, I wrote to you
again. I was in university, sitting in a cafeteria full of people,
looking up at the television monitors and trying
not to think about that old radio program they made from
The War of the Worlds.

I wrote you the following letter, there in the cafeteria: "Dear RAND, right now I feel like I felt in the Museum of Modern Art, looking at those paintings. I know that they must mean something. I know that there must be some reason for them. But I can't see it. All I see is a mess. Those are people jumping from the windows. That is too high up."

And you sent the letter back then, too, RAND. But I understand. The world is full of letters, pointing fingers at the problems, at faults, without suggesting a solution. This letter is a solution.

Why not fake every disaster? Empty planes look just the same on TV. Nobody needs to know the passengers are safe. Empty buildings. Robot jumpers. You could have put a look-alike dummy of my brother on his skateboard in front of a robot drunk driver. It was nighttime, who would know? Fake everyone's death for the cameras, but let them live.

Give me the moon, RAND. I can be your backup plan. We can start a secret lunar colony for the secret survivors! A place where nothing dies, where smiles are free. There won't be any war or pollution or over-population. Every night at six we'll listen to *The Shadow*, and later on there'll be a comedy for mom and dad.

It's Christmas Eve. We could have a roaring fire.

Yours,
Joey Comeau

Dear Gillette,

Do you remember when you were the best a man could get? Before you decided that the best that men could get were faces as soft as baby bottoms? Before you decided that being a man meant being a woman? You need to go back to your roots, Gillette. Forget these gaudy lozenge shaped miracles of modern technology. Bring back the straight razor. That was a product.

You want dangerous? Forget about drunk businessmen and speeding cars. You want Gillette razors against a businessman's throat in an alley. Gillette razors hidden in the mouths of inmates. Hidden under their skin. Scabbed over. Finally dug out with dirty fingers in the dark.

You want coming of age? That has nothing to do with a clean shave. You want a young boy sneaking into his stepfather's bathroom. Sneaking a razor from the box. Hiding it in the brim of his baseball cap. Riding his bike hard and fast to meet his best friend in the woods. A Gillette razor digging into their palms. That one handshake. Blood brothers. You want romance? Nobody gives a fuck about kisses. Gillette razors in bed, cutting while they move against one another. Both of them tearing open, bright and bleeding, eyes wide. Sex, Gillette. Sex.

They're going to buy your razor and shave and go to work, sure, but they're going to buy it because they know they're animals inside. They don't want smiling clean faces. They want blood swirling down the drain. You're selling a product to men who have no other way of touching that part of themselves, the suicide and the murder and the rape.

I can help.

Joey Comeau

Dear Parker Brothers,

Last night I dreamed my brother and I were hanging out at a party, trying to drink as many little bottles of alcohol as possible. We were hoping to get very drunk without anyone noticing. Then I was trying to explain to Adrian how we had the exact same Muppets toothbrush. He was pissed because someone gave him a stale sandwich. All of the other models were sitting around in a classroom, laughing and talking. We were models? Someone was talking about waves. We could hear the waves crashing on the rocks. The whole room went dark, and a girl in the middle was lit from above. Her skin was rotted and bloody black and she looked right at me and she said, very calmly, "A catastrophe is coming."

I have never designed a board game before, but I think I'd be good at it. You roll the dice and make your move. How hard can it be? All you need is a theme. What about disaster? I like that. It's harrowing without being too immediate. Those things happen to other people.

Joey Comeau

Dear Paramount Pictures,

I want to write horror movies. When I was a kid, I was terrified of horror movies. I remember watching *Pet Sematary* four times before I ever saw more than a flash of the dead guy. I hid underneath a blanket every time anything happened, every time the music came up. I covered my ears.

I liked being scared, though. My grandparents owned a farm, and my brother Adrian and I used to sneak out to the barn in the middle of the night. My grandfather used that barn to store the tractor. It used to be a real barn, though. It was left over from when there had been a farm, not just a vineyard back there. It was old and broken down and perfect for us.

Adrian and I went in there with our flashlights, and there was a room underneath the hayloft. It was small and dark and slick and there were no windows. It was a room where your imagination became full of snorting stomping animals all wet with sweat. Even in the middle of the day, that room was black like horse eyes.

One of us would sit outside and the other would go in, without his flashlight, and see how long he could stand to be alone in that black room. It wasn't the sort of game that anybody won or lost.

I've thought about this a lot, Paramount. I want to write horror movies that scare you, but leave you with the feeling that your brother is right outside the door, waiting, flashlight in hand.

Only, when you call out, there's no answer. And the barn is empty, like your stomach.

Joey Comeau

Dear Bell Canada,

Thank you for taking the time to review my resume. I have to apologize for the bluntness of this cover letter. I need your help. I think the Internet is trying to kill me. It is only through this channel, this job application, that I have any chance of fooling it into letting my message get through.

I spent six hours online this morning, reading job postings and writing terrible cover letters, and having shallow conversations with a dozen of my friends. They kept asking, "How do you feel?" and posting the little hug icon from instant messenger. When was the last time I really paid attention to a conversation? I have all these old emails from my brother, and none of them say anything.

He ended every one with, "Love yah, bro." I've read it so many times today.

I'm multitasking all the time now. I can do a hundred different things at once, and at the end of the day I can't remember any of them. I honestly can't remember.

It's your fault. The Internet has tendrils in millions of homes, all through the country. You feed it. And I understand why you feed it, why you're doing this. You get thirty dollars a month for every home, for every connection. You're feeding it, but you're getting fat, too. Only, it can't go on. I can't let you profit from the lives of my friends and family.

You have to tell me where it lives. If I can find the head, the heart, the brain, I can destroy it. I can set everyone free with one small act of violence. I need to burn the Internet to the ground. I need to find out if it has had a chance to lay eggs yet.

Have you had trouble breathing lately? When was your last x-ray? There could be eggs anywhere in your body. I have to tear out its backbone. I have to clean your server rooms with fire. If I am in the computers as an employee, it won't see me coming, gasoline can in hand.

Hire me.

Joey Comeau

Dear Queen Elizabeth Hospital,

I'm applying for the position of systems analyst in the
Transplantation Services department of your hospital, as
advertised on the Internet. I'm currently working as a
systems analyst for Ford Motor Company of Canada, but I
am looking to make the transition to medicine, and I am
including my resume for your review. I have always had a
strong interest in medicine, and it is that interest which
originally attracted me to the sciences. Circumstances led
me to computer science, but it seems that now I am being
given the chance to follow my original dreams. I can leave
behind the cold and lifeless world of automotive
manufacturing, and embrace the emotionally satisfying
warmth of health care.

I know it won't be an easy transition, and this is why I am
applying to your hospital. Your hospital is the perfect
balance of medicine and assembly line. I can work with
bodies, but won't be expected to treat them as people. Over
time, of course, I might learn to understand human emotion
and move on to another hospital where that is more
appropriate, but in the meantime I think you will find my
qualifications and skills very useful.

As my resume indicates, my duties at Ford have included
leading the programming team in charge of assembly line
robotics. My experience taught me about the maximum
speed and force with which you could have the robot insert
a new part without damaging a vehicle's chassis. I feel this

experience will translate almost seamlessly to transplantation services, and I think you will agree.

While at Ford I've also led a team in designing a system for locating defects in the assembly line vehicles. It is a waste of resources and time to assemble vehicles that are not up to standard, and I wonder if this philosophy might not be something that the medical world is ready to embrace.

What it all comes down to is this: I am a resourceful and innovative programmer. I am not afraid of learning new things, and I know when trial and error is a faster way to get something done than research. I can be a hard taskmaster to those beneath me in the chain of command, but the results of that show in my production figures.

I believe that I would make a vital and innovative member of your team. Too often industries are the victims of over-specialization, and I feel that my breadth of experience and attitudes toward transplantation services would give your department the distinction that it may well require.

Yours in anticipation,

Joey Comeau

Dear Goodyear,

I'd like a job, please. You probably don't hire strangers. I used to climb mountains of your tires in my grandfather's salvage yard. My name's Joey Comeau. There. Now we aren't strangers anymore.

It's Joey, not Joe or Joseph. My grandfather was Joe Comeau, and Joseph is my mother's name for me, but I have always been Joey. I worry sometimes that it's a childish name. Would a "Joe" tell jokes in bed, perform puppet shows after sex, and give every body part a different high-pitched voice? It seems unlikely. The names we choose for ourselves aren't meaningless. They're self-fulfilling prophecies.

So, I'm Joey and I will never be Joe. When my grandfather died, I lost my chance to know him as anything more than a kiss on the cheek and a drive to the video store. I remember his oxygen tank, and his chair in the living room. Every night at seven or eight o'clock my grandmother would move to the kitchen and pour herself a glass of wine from a box, because it was time for wrestling and the TV was his for hours. Their furniture was old and dark brown, and it hid dimes and nickels. My grandmother lives in another city now, with new furniture, and I wonder if every night at seven or eight o'clock, she still finds something else to do. She hated wrestling.

I remember how even after he sold the salvage yard, he ran an alternator rebuilding shop out of the garage. He lost money, and I think it worried my grandmother, but he always had something to do. When we did talk, it was so I could help him with his parts database on the computer. I remember how excited he was with the features, the index and photographs, and how he never seemed frustrated when something went wrong with the program. He would call me and tell me the error message to see if I could help. I was always surprised by the call.

My brother Adrian lived with them for a while, after he was kicked out of our house. Way out in Dartmouth, an hour from the nearest bus stop. Every day he would get a drive into town, or at least to the ferry, with our grandfather. When he was living there I'm sure that things weren't perfect, but Adrian formed a closer relationship with my grandmother. That's what I was jealous of at the time. He told me once that she said he was her favourite grandson. I understand that now. How nice would it be, after your children are gone, to have your grandson living with you?

My grandfather was driving Adrian into Halifax a few years ago, and it was either rainy or snowy. I can't remember. A man staggered into the street, drunk, and they hit him. I remember Adrian telling me about sitting quietly in the car, my grandfather crying, while they waited for the ambulance.

What a strange thing to be jealous of.

Joey Comeau

Dear MIT,

I am writing to apply for a position as researcher in your Linguistics department. I would like to focus on language and memory, specifically the language of nostalgia. I have been trying to write down my memories and it's all such bullshit. Is nostalgia like kittens? Does it make our language stupid? OH MY GOODNESS YOU'RE A KITTY!

I remember the woman with brown hair who taught me grade four; she left halfway through the year. I loved her. Her name started with an M. Mrs. Munroe? I can't remember. I can remember the shape of that room, and the view from my seat out the window. That window had a grate on it, and all class I would just stare. Focus on the trees, focus on the grate. Focus on the trees, focus on the grate. Back and forth. I remember sitting in the back of her classroom and reading science fiction books. I almost failed that year. I almost failed every year. I can't remember her face.

It doesn't really bother me that I can't remember, though. It was a long time ago, and it's not important. Sometimes it's nice to look back and only remember little bits. My memories of that school, of being that young, are like a weird slideshow.

I remember how excited I got when the Scholastic book fair came to our library. I went through the catalogues again and again, noting which books I wanted to buy. Then, when the day finally came, I would spend forever going from table to table, trying to choose.

I remember the girl's bathroom and not the boy's. I only went in once. The showers had seats. I remember that my best friend waited on the field behind the school for another friend of mine, and he hit him in the leg with his baseball bat. This was elementary school.

So much violence.

I remember both their names, but not their faces.

There must be a way we can talk about the past so that it's more than just the past. Everything that has happened or will happen exists together. Just at different times. People die, but that isn't any different from the edge of a table. The table is still there. It just doesn't stretch that far.

I am not saying any of this right.

I remember we went on a camping field trip and I was sent home. I remember screaming and kicking while someone carried me. I remember my brother got his foot crushed in a gate out behind our school. It was recess. He always wore that red sweater. I remember how quiet everything seemed and how nobody would let me near him.

Joey Comeau

Dear New York Times,

Thank you for taking the time to review my resume. I am writing to apply for the position as editor, and I'm certain that upon closer examination you will find that my enclosed resume demonstrates my ability as an editor perhaps more accurately than it describes my experience in the field. I mean simply that any difference between the results of a background check and the employment history I have delineated should be taken as an example of my skills.

My skills as an editor extend beyond my job history to encompass the whole of my past. A stint in juvenile hall adds a much-needed bit of excitement to a childhood I can barely remember. I don't mean to imply that I'm a revisionist. I was never a revisionist. I won awards. I dated the prettiest girls.

Like, once, in college. I met a pretty girl who was a lesbian. Everyone told me that it would just break my heart to fall in love with her, that I was wasting my time, that I was asking for trouble. Well, within a week she had fallen for me. And there was no trouble at all. Her love for me overwhelmed her and she forgot all about her distaste for the immediate facts of the matter (if you will). We're still happily married. We have kids. Two, I guess. A boy and a girl. Handsome and pretty. It wasn't even hard.

My brother was never hit by a car, and the last time we spoke (just this morning) he said he loved me, and that he'd had a nightmare where he told me to go fuck myself over something as stupid as a rent cheque, and then died before he could apologize. He said that when he woke up he felt really bad about that, and I said, "It's okay, man! The important thing is that we love and respect each other and that you're still alive! I love you, bro."

We had a pretty good laugh about that, and then we got wicked drunk. I will make a very good editor for your company, whether you hire me or not.

Joey Comeau

Dear Mister President,

I would like to apply for a job as your Chief Environmental Advisor. Everyone is so afraid all the time. Of dying. The world is running out of oil, or ozone, or patience. We're all doomed. I can't read the newspaper anymore. I like to listen to stories about cats with one crooked fang that sticks up, about dogs who drool when they're happy. Why don't they have that in the newspaper? Why don't they have stories about drunk drivers who hit young men, and afterwards everybody laughs with nervous relief. They say, "Man, that could have gone much worse! Haha, we dodged a bullet there. Can I buy you a drink?"

Sure, everything falls apart. Love is like that, too. Even family is like that. But I'd like to quote Mr. Mitch Hedberg, if I may: "A girl asked me if I drink red wine. I said yes and she asked, 'But doesn't it give you a headache?' And I said, 'Sure . . . EVENTUALLY.'" Pause for effect. "'But the first and the middle parts are amazing.'"

Everything falls apart, and it fucking sucks and we're all going to be in those wooden boxes eventually. Pause for effect. But the first and the middle parts are amazing!

Yours,

Joey Comeau

Dear Nintendo,

Thank you for taking the time to consider my resume. I am writing to apply for the position of game designer. We have a chance here to help children experience games that are more true to life than ever before. Computer graphics have improved and improved and improved, and some day soon we're going to have to ask ourselves where we can go next in our search for realism.

We need virtual pet games where you clean and feed and love your furry little friend, but where that car still comes out of nowhere so smoothly, a god of aerodynamics and passenger safety. Where your mother says, "Good thing we kept this." And she takes a shoe box down from your closet. Where you hear your father's quiet joke that night, when he thinks you are asleep.

We need an airport simulator, where the planes carry your whole family from A to B, job to job, and dad still drinks in the shower when you have to pee. Your older sister still comes home at three in the morning and wakes you up so she can sit on the edge of your bed and cry. Where you try to make friends faster at each new school, so you tell jokes even though you don't know anybody and nobody gets them. Everybody says you're the weird new kid. So at the next school you don't say anything at all and then you're the weird quiet kid. The plane touches down and you all lean forward in your seats because of inertia, and again and again someone says, "I hate to fly."

We need a new Mario game where you rescue the princess in the first ten minutes, and for the rest of the game you try to push down that sick feeling in your stomach telling you she's "damaged goods," a concept detailed again and again in the profoundly sex-negative instruction booklet, and when Luigi makes a crack about her and Bowser, you break his nose and immediately regret it. Peach asks you, in the quiet of her mushroom castle bedroom, "Do you still love me?" and you pretend to be asleep. You press the A button rhythmically, to control your breath, to keep it even.

Yours,

Joey Comeau

part two.

overqualifiec

Dear Apple,

I am writing to apply for a position with your company, and I am including my resume for your review. It outlines my experience as a computer programmer in the field of natural language processing.

Late at night, drunk, our language changes. In the day, I simply eat a piece of fruit, but late at night, while my girlfriend Susan sleeps, I tell another woman how I am piercing the skin with my teeth. Then I am cutting flesh from it and laying those pieces on my tongue. I am imagining that its flavors are hers.

We can train the computer to recognize these changes. Your connection can be suspended for your own good, long before you hit send. Txt Msging and email are the new drunk dialing, and we can help protect users from themselves. We can protect them from their own natural inclinations to lewdness, regret, longing, desperation. Imagine a robot operator listening to your calls, robot finger at the ready, waiting to disconnect you when you call at 4 a.m. to say you should never have let her go, that you think about her breasts sometimes, about that hollow where her neck cups up behind her ear? I'm sorry that I let you go. I should have followed. I can't bear to think of you with him, piercing and laying his flesh on your — DISCONNECT.

There are reasons why we can't just do what we want. Sometimes, in the middle of the night, I am suddenly certain that I will die. My brother was a year and a half younger than me. He was charming and all of the girls loved him. Now he's dead. A drunk driver came out of nowhere and he is dead. And I will die. I will die and Susan is the last girl. I sit on the bed beside her while she sleeps and I think, "This is the last girl." But that's not as scary as it seems, is it? Love is important. But this is the last girl I will love, too. That's scarier. My mind goes in circles, and then I go and sit down in front of the computer, Apple. That's where I need your protection.

We can make the world a better place for the broken.

Joey Comeau

Dear Credico,

I am writing to apply for the position of Sales Rep. I'm located in the city of Halifax, where your ad says you are currently recruiting, and I am including my resume for your review. My resume details my sales experience, and I assure you that I am the person for this position.

Sometimes I think dent-resistant side panels are a waste of money, but then I remember ladies be always throwing themselves at my car, and titties can wreak havoc on a paint job. When it's warm, women like to take their titties out for a walk. You never see them in the winter, but in the hot months I guess their titties just start scratching at the door and yowling, and they need to be appeased.

Titties can be like rabid fucking animals, man. They claw at the carpet and they tear shirts down to the navel. I am an animal too. I can't stop thinking about them. Their titty pheromones get stuck in my head. They get in through my face. What I am supposed to be thinking about? A house? Two and a half children? A nice quiet family plot on a hill down at the graveyard?

TITTIES TITTIES TITTIES.

FUCK.

Yours,

Joey Comeau

Dear Yahoo,

Thank you for taking the time to review my resume. In addition, I have attached transcriptions of some of my most recent games on your online Yahoo Chess server. I believe that my ability and skill as an analyst and strategist in the games section of Yahoo.com will demonstrate that I'm a perfect fit with your company. It is worth noting, before you review this material, that I lost every time. The real strategy lies in the chat transcripts that accompany each game.

I played under the fake name Trish Highsmith, and when pressed for information about myself I supplied intriguing but vague details. I pretended to be a fourteen-year-old lesbian. Some days I claimed to have relationship problems. I pretended to be a girl who was learning to play chess so that she could beat her girlfriend at the game. I could have said anything, as long as I was a girl. I figured people would be more likely to give me pointers if I were a lady. Instead, things got out of hand.

Trish_Highsmith: I'm the bass player in a band, and I'm thinking of studying the philosophy of history at the graduate level. What can we know? Are there degrees of certainty about our beliefs regarding the past? Is direct observation the only truth we have? I refuse to believe that. Is history just a joke? I just don't know what to think.

RNorth_dinocok: Do you have a boyfriend?
RNorth_dinocok: What color are your underwears?

RNorth_dinocok: What do you look like?
RNorth_dinocok: You seem really nice.

or

Trish _Highsmith: That was an awful move! Sorry, I am practising my openings, and sometimes I worry too much about making the move I remember instead of watching where you're moving and taking that into consideration.

MSaturday_Stud_Stud: What do your undies look like?
MSaturday_Stud_Stud: Show me your pussy.
MSaturday_Stud_Stud: Checkmate.

Actually, halfway through writing this email, I realized there is no connection between strategy and my actions. These transcriptions don't show my skill as an analyst. On reflection, they show only that I like to pretend to be a girl on Yahoo Chess so I can talk dirty with other men.

Please hire me?

Yours,

Joey Comeau

Dear Financial Services Firm,

Thank you for taking the time to review my application for a position conducting telephone surveys for your company. My resume lists my recent professional work in the field, but the formal structure of a resume doesn't provide room to discuss the personal nature of my first experiences with telephone surveys.

When I was eight years old I began to experiment with crank calling. A staple of mine was, "Hello, is your refrigerator running?" and then, "Well you'd better go and catch it!" I did not invent this joke. I did invent: "Hello. You fuck dogs!"

When the boys at school began to talk about sex, I felt stupid. I had no idea what they were talking about. So I called a number at random. A woman answered.

"Hello?"

"Is your refrigerator running?"

"It is," she said.

"What's a clitoris?"

There are some questions a dictionary can't answer. The Internet could have told me what a clitoris was. I don't think any definition would have explained quite what Jeff meant when he wiggled his fingers as he said it. People will always be our best source of information. Anyway, I'm not legally allowed to call strangers anymore. But if I worked for you, it would be okay again!

"Hello, I'm calling on behalf of Financial Services Firm. Do you have a moment for a couple of questions? Do you ever worry that maybe you don't have as much time as you thought? What about the things you haven't done yet? I don't mean kayaking or bungee jumping. I mean the girl with the dark glasses and the facial tattoo on the subway. I mean the woman who guides tours at the museum who has the crazy perfect laugh. I mean that man in my building who seems to carry his hockey stick everywhere. I have a girlfriend, Susan, and I love her. But it drives me crazy to see them and to know that I can't touch them. I won't ever be surprised by them. Do you get this way?"

Anyway, I could ask the questions that you wanted as well!

Joey Comeau

Dear Hallmark,

Mother's Day is fine, I guess. Except some people have lost their mothers. And some people have lost their fathers. Not everyone has family. You want a holiday with wider appeal. Well, we all have strangers on the edges of our lives. We can all be secret admirers.

Look around the next time you're at the mall. Or look online. Social networking sites. The Internet is full of people to secretly admire. I went online this morning and fell in love a dozen times.

There's a girl who makes detailed maps of her neighbourhood and she knows a boy who hates Allen Ginsberg — except for one line that he thinks is perfect. He has crooked eyes and takes all these pictures of balls bouncing. That is his obsession, bouncing rubber balls. He knows a girl who, in every picture, is pulling her shirt up to show off her belly. Every picture. "What's up? A camera? Yeah yeah. Let me get my belly out." She looks so happy just to be here. She knows a trashy girl in a tank top, wearing a little too much makeup, who is out drinking with her sorority friends in every picture. This girl has bleached blonde hair and only one interest: *Carnival of Souls* (1962).

What ever happened to secret admirers? Are they just stalkers now? If you notice someone, if you pay too much attention, that's weird. All of a sudden you're that guy who sits on the bench in the mall, right in front of the store where she works, staring inside all day. Or, worse, you're the guy who keeps going in. The guy with the Orange Julius who keeps saying, "I'm just browsing."

But I've never been able to just walk up to a pretty girl and start talking. My brother used to do that. Charm was his specialty. The closest I can come is writing notes. I write notes to strangers while my girlfriend is at work.

"You have the best laugh I have ever heard. The only thing I know about you is that you work with maps and you always take the second straw from the dispenser — I do that too!"

You need a new holiday, Hallmark.

International Stalker Day.

Joey Comeau

Dear Aliant Zinc,

I am writing to apply for the position of bookkeeper. Attached, you will find my resume, and a list of my qualifications. I have been keeping books for four years now, and I am never going to give them back.

The first book I ever kept was *A Strange Manuscript Found in a Copper Cylinder*. A lady friend lent the book to me just after we'd met, when we were first exposing our tastes to one another. She smiled, handed me the book and said, "These words will change the way you think about your life," or something like that. I don't really remember. I just remember the way that book felt in my hand. It belonged there.

When I was a child I had a mild case of obsessive-compulsive disorder, and this feeling was like that. It was satisfying the way counting the hairs on the other children during naptime was satisfying. It was like a nail being driven into a board.

When a week had gone by, my lady friend asked, "Have you finished with my book yet?"

I shook my head. "No," I said, "but I'm finished with you."

That was how it started. That was the beginning of my library. Keeping books became so much more satisfying than orgasms had ever been. Adding to my bookshelves was more exciting than ridiculous underwear or clumsy sexual innuendo. Every girl would lend me a book or two, and I would slide it onto my bookshelf and write them a polite note.

"Lisa, please do not stop by anymore."

"Allison, no thanks."

After a few months, I realized that I needed a second bookshelf. My collection was growing rapidly. Whenever I talked to my mother, she wanted to talk about my fear of commitment. She was worried, she said, that I had been acting differently since my brother's death. She said I was always running from women who were perfect for me.

But romance was Adrian's thing. There won't be twenty sobbing girls at my funeral, none of them looking at one another, each clutching a handkerchief.

"Well, what was wrong with that pretty girl with the punk rock hair?" my mother said. "She seemed nice enough."

"She owned every single Tom Clancy novel," I said. "But love doesn't last forever."

Yours,

Joey Comeau

Dear Airwalk,

Sometimes it feels good to fall off your skateboard. It hurts like a fucker, and your body aches and you can't stop smiling.

Sometimes it feels good to go out and skate and climb and run until you're exhausted, miles away from home. You didn't plan on ending up somewhere so far away. You just did what your body wanted.

I've started to take disasters as good omens, like the death card in tarot decks. I've started to read the newspaper like people read chicken bones. Somewhere in that mess, you can tell the future. Where did they find her body? On the second floor? Don't invest in any new business opportunities this week. A bomb went off in the subway north of the main line, not south. That's a good sign. The death count was an odd number. Now is the time for a new love in your life.

I want a piece of everything today. Do you get like this? I feel sure that every stranger would be the perfect surprise in bed. Out of nowhere they would spit in my face, would mention Patricia Highsmith. They would smile at the exact wrong moment and that moment would be all I remembered. I've been meeting people's eyes on the street. I've been writing pornography to be read out loud. I want to wear a sign all the time around my neck that says, "Yes."

Yours,

Joey Comeau

Dear Greenpeace,

I have been thinking about sex. I don't think there's anything wrong with that. It's almost September, and soon fall will be here. I don't know what you're doing today, but maybe you would rather be thinking about sex, too. This morning I woke up and remembered an embarrassing sex story. Everyone has embarrassing sex stories, I hope.

My girlfriend Susan and I were in bed together, masturbating. We had just met. Everything was exciting and terrible. She was on her back, naked, touching herself, and I was above her, mostly naked, doing the same. I was eighteen or nineteen years old, and all I could think about was coming on her breasts. You know, like on the Internet. I think, probably, I was saying something to that effect. I wasn't mentioning the Internet, of course, but I was saying, "I'm going to come on you. I'm going to come on you."

I'm classy like that.

I don't remember how she felt about the whole coming-on-her idea, actually, but I can tell you that I was very excited about it. I was almost lying on top of her. I was leaned forward so far. So when I felt my orgasm coming, I looked down between us to watch for the come shot.

I came in my own eye. It was like a 3D movie gone terribly wrong, and it stung. I started clawing at my face. Susan laughed and laughed while I tried frantically to wipe my eye clean. She was curled up naked on the bed, laughing so hard there were tears. I started laughing too. I couldn't help it. We both laughed until it hurt, until the muscles in our cheeks were sore from smiling, and then we looked up at her ceiling, on our backs, exhausted. For the rest of that afternoon, every once in a while one of us would start laughing again and then so would the other.

I thought about that after we fought tonight. I get so confused in my head. I almost left her, but that isn't what I want. I want to sleep with other women, yes, but I want Susan, too. She is strong and sexy and just as surprising as those strangers. I don't want them instead of her. Maybe there is a way I can have both. I don't know. I do know that this love is important.

When the end comes, when the ice caps melt and the seas boil and the sky falls, I won't want to be hiding in some stranger's bathroom.

I will want Susan's hand in mine.

Yours truly,

Joey Comeau

Dear Sirs or Madams!

I hope you will consider me for a position with Nova Magnetics. My resume details my experience with magnet technical sales, but I would like to take some time to explain my other qualifications as well. When I was a child I accidentally swallowed a small kitten-shaped fridge magnet. It's still inside me, lodged in my intestine somewhere, and I hope to God that it stays there. It gives me special powers.

Do you know anyone who can see perfectly in the dark? Cats can do it. Owls. Heck, my little brother had abnormally good night vision, God rest his soul. But do you know anyone who goes completely blind if the sun even goes behind a cloud?

Well you do now.

And that's the least of my powers — I have others. For example, I have a form of ESP that allows me to consistently pick losing lottery numbers, and generally make poor life choices. I consistently make poor life choices. I had a shirt made up that says, "I consistently make poor life choices." The shirt was not very popular. I can come up with unpopular t-shirt slogans on the spot.

"Kiss me, I have no night vision."

"This womb drops babies!"

And, my least popular shirt, "Threesome?"

I wore this one on a date with my girlfriend, Susan. The date did not go well.

"Come on," I said.

"Nope," she said.

I am not a freak because I want to sleep with two chicks at the same time. That is perfectly normal! I am a freak because there is a magnet shaped like a kitten stuck inside me. I would love to discuss this position further. Please call. I am free all the time now.

Yours,

Joey Comeau

Dear Hallmark,

Thank you for taking the time to review my greeting card ideas.

Idea #1

Front cover is a to-do list, scrawled on a notepad. The text reads: "Do dishes. Pick up light bulbs. Tell my lady that she means the world to me." Inside text: "Apologize for pressuring her into a threesome."

Idea #2

Front cover is a picture of a puppy dog with big, sad eyes. A Golden Retriever, maybe. Some breed that everyone loves, something vulnerable. The text on the front reads: "You think love has to last forever for it to be real. You think it isn't true love unless it lasts until one of us is dead." Inside text: "That isn't love. That's dog fighting."

Idea #3

Front cover is a pretty butterfly, pinned under glass. The text reads, "I love you." There is no inside text.

Yours,

Joey Comeau

Dear Easy Rider Tours,

I am writing to submit my application for the position of bicycle tour guide, and I am including my resume for your review. It outlines my years of experience with leading tours in general, and with leading bicycle tours in particular. I look forward to lending my individual brand of tour innovation to your company.

The chance to lead a tour of Nova Scotia and Prince Edward Island is an exciting opportunity for me. For years I have been developing a set of specialized theme tours of these two great provinces, and the chance to implement them with busloads of unsuspecting tourists is like a gift from heaven.

I know that it's difficult to assess potential tours based simply on a description, and so I have prepared a mock script of my "Nova Scotia Tour of Joey's Ex-lovers," even though I feel it would be better to work unscripted — to maintain a level of spontaneity tourists would likely appreciate. Here is a small sampling of the planned tour.

Stop number one: I never thought it would be like this.

"Coming up on the left, we find the bakery where my very first girlfriend works. Laura. When we were fourteen, we both got really drunk and had sex. Raised, as I was, with a strong sense of religious virtue, I stumbled out of her house, crying. I never thought . . . hang on, here she is."

At this point I pull the megaphone out of my bag.

"HOW ARE YOU TODAY, HARLOT? OFF TO STEAL THE INNOCENCE OF ANOTHER CONFUSED CHILD? YOU WILL BURN IN HELL FOR WHAT YOU DID TO ME!"

I am hoping she won't laugh at me again.

Stop number six: Maybe if you shaved your legs?

"And here we have another old girlfriend's house. Emma, who gave me, for my birthday, a copy of *Oral Sex Tips for Men*. What the fuck is that all about?" I pull out the megaphone.

"IT'S NOT BECAUSE I DIDN'T KNOW HOW, EMMA. IT'S BECAUSE I'M SAVING THAT FOR A GIRL I REALLY LOVE. YOU WERE JUST HELPING ME KILL TIME. YOU'RE LIKE INTERNET PORNOGRAPHY, BUT CHEAPER."

Stop number ten: Susan's house.

Megaphone: "Hello Susan. I'm not disturbing your sleep, am I? I'd feel terrible about that. I mean, I've already inconvenienced you so much, what with my brother dying while you were trying to finish out your year at college. I know you probably don't have the energy for this anymore. Everything is so hard. Life is such a disaster, and my weird sex requests were the last straw. Well, don't you worry! You left and that's fine. I don't want you back. You're free.

"And I'll tell you what. I'm going to ride my bike around all night and feel the wind and the stars and the quiet, and life is going to be perfect again, and when I come home I am going to come home somewhere else."

This is just a small sampling of the sort of tours I've worked out. I can help elevate the tourism business from its stagnant state to the exciting status it deserves, and life really will be perfect again. I look forward to hearing from you about this position.

Joey Comeau

Dear General Electric,

I am applying for a position as an engineer. Your line of water heaters is flawed, but I think these flaws are important. I am worried that you will hire someone else, someone who will identify those flaws and correct them.

Our apartment flooded last month. The water heater burst. Water came seeping out from under the door of the furnace room. This was late at night. It was like a Japanese horror movie. I thought, at first, that Susan had spilled a glass of water on the floor by the desk. Then it kept coming, then more. We moved the desks, the computers, everything. It kept pouring into the room. The water came pouring out from under the door, and then from the wall beside it. Soon the carpet there was black.

"Don't open that door," Susan said. She could tell we were in a horror movie, too. She sounded terrified and irritated at the same time. When I opened the door it all flooded in. *Whoosh*. It was deep inside. It looked like it went down forever, but maybe that was just the light.

I was half-naked and bewildered. Susan was so angry. Her pants and socks were soaked. I remember I made a joke about skinny-dipping. I've never actually been skinny-dipping. They do it in books.

The problem with skinny-dipping is you pretty much have to go at night. The problem with night swimming is the darkness. The dark water and the dark all around, where you can hear the bugs but can't see them. I hate swimming at night. I always think of hands underneath me. I always think of Jason Voorhees, a thick dead man in a hockey mask chained to the bottom of the lake, hands reaching up.

I am glad that our water heater broke. It was an adventure and now it's a weird and haunted memory. Black water and anger. The industrial fan made awful noises all night. My dreams were messed up. I remember Susan was banging dishes around in the kitchen when I woke. She always said she didn't do that on purpose, but I don't know. She wanted me to know when she was angry. I should have paid more attention. I can't seem to hold on to anyone.

Joey Comeau

part three.

overqualified

Dear Samsonite,

I found an old suitcase in my grandmother's basement two weeks ago. I was downstairs, to get away from our awkward conversation. I try to speak French and she answers me in English. She tells me, "No, you don't want to learn Acadian. It's not even real French." This isn't how I imagined it would be. She wants to help, I think. But I'm having a hard time here. So I've been going through the stored boxes in the basement, and I found an old suitcase. It was grey and dusty, and it had my grandfather's initials. My initials. JC. I pulled it out into the centre of the room and set it down. I pulled hard at the old zipper, which went all the way around, and when I flipped open the top there was a ladder leading down into the floor. Something near the bottom was flickering.

I climbed down slowly, not really believing what was going on, scared of what I might find, but unable to resist. I climbed down and down into the dark. The walls were warm and soft and I tried not to touch them.

My grandfather was sitting alone in a room down there, watching wrestling on the television. The iron lung sat unused in the corner of the room. I stood there and watched with him while men lifted one another into the air and bounced off the blue mat together. During the commercial, he looked up and smiled at me. He held his glass out, and I took it to the kitchen and filled it with wine. He tousled my hair and then turned back to the TV. There were tunnels leading off into other rooms.

My great aunt, sewing me costumes. Her budgie, under the floor, in a shoe box, singing along to the machine. I tried on the big billowing pumpkin costume she offered, and it fit.

"I have another one here for your little brother," she told me. "Go fetch him, will you?"

In the next room, Adrian sat on the floor, Nintendo controller in hand. I picked up the other controller. The thing about playing Mortal Kombat with Adrian was how cheap he was. He would get you into a corner and just sweep kick you again and again, and your character had no time to react. There was no window of opportunity. He kicked and kicked and I mashed the buttons and cursed and Adrian just laughed and laughed. When my character was dead, I said, "Fuck, I died." Adrian turned to me and smiled.

I wandered more. My first dog, Sarah, who really did go to live on a farm — but died there anyway. My great grandmother and her silver dollars. You can get lost down there in those tunnels. It took a long time for me to find my way back to the ladder. I started climbing. A few rungs back up toward the basement, I felt my grandfather's hand on my ankle. He was out of his chair, looking up. He held out his wine glass for me. Upstairs, two weeks had gone by. Memories are like everything else. They're a trap.

Joey Comeau

Dear American Express,

I got a letter by registered mail today, threatening me about money. I owe more than forty thousand dollars for student loans. I also owe for credit cards, the power bill, the telephone. When my brother got hurt, I let everything slide. Now when I read these threats I feel like I am underwater, and going deeper and deeper and then — POP! — everything is fine again. The important thing is living. My stepfather says my debt will double in ten years. And then in ten years it will double again. Maybe. And maybe in ten years that will double. That sounds frightening, I guess, except that I'm not going to live forever, am I? There's a flaw in their math. Forty thousand times two is eighty thousand times two is one hundred and sixty thousand times two is nothing.

Anyway, have you got any jobs?

Joey Comeau

Dear Spherion,

I am writing to apply for a position as corporate collections representative. Corporations have been collecting from me for years. So I have started calling them. I'm tired of being afraid. It's time they were afraid of me.

8 a.m.

"Hi, is MasterCard there?"

"This is MasterCard, who is this?"

"Good morning. This is Joey calling. If you don't make your minimum payment . . ."

They hang up on me.

But I'm a motivated worker. I've devised a campaign of terror. I want to wake MasterCard up at three in the morning and make veiled little threats about their credit rating. Every day they'll find themselves interrupted in the middle of breakfast, lunch, and dinner. I'll make McDonald's get up from its veggie stir-fry and come to the phone.

And I won't take any shit.

"Don't you people have any respect?" Sony will say. "We're trying to eat. We will pay when we pay." They'll hang up. I'll call right back.

"That's a pretty little dog you have out in the yard, Sony," I'll say. "I bet a dog like that is expensive to feed. If you're having trouble making your payments, maybe there's something we can do to help."

And when the woman on the other end of the phone tells me, "MasterCard doesn't live here anymore. I think she died." I'll smile.

"She looked pretty healthy for a dead woman this morning," I'll say, "when she was climbing out of bed with VISA's husband. At least, I think she did. It's so hard to tell with photographs."

This is a field in which I can distinguish myself. I would be an asset to your company and I look forward to hearing from you about this position.

Joey Comeau

Dear NYPD,

I'd like to be a police officer, please. I could be a police officer from the Great White North. An Aboriginal cop! I found my Aboriginal status card today. It was hidden in a drawer. Joseph Mitchell Comeau, Eastern Woodland Métis Nation of Nova Scotia! *Le pays boisé de l'est Nouvelle-Écosse!* My status card makes me happy, but is pretty much just a piece of paper. It's one of those small items that just cheer you up. It looks like it was printed out on a crappy dot matrix printer and home-laminated, which it probably was. Whenever anyone makes a crack about how homemade it looks, I say, "Oh I'm sorry. My people don't use the white man's technology effectively enough for you?"

My grandmother had Adrian and me apply for the cards a couple years ago, in the hopes that we would be able to get financial assistance going through university for being First Nations. The only information I could find, though, said that the Canadian Government didn't recognize Métis as being real in'jun!

Maybe I'm not even allowed to say in'jun, being only Métis.

I have Adrian's status card in a box under my bed. I have his motorcycle licence and his Métis card and a half-full bottle of painkillers and his birth certificate. He used to love Indian jokes. What do you want to do tonight, Adrian? Well, let's get a garbage bag full of gasoline to huff, Joey. Let's tie some feathers to our heads. Gotta stay true to our roots.

At night it's too warm, so I turn the heat down and when I wake up in the morning I am waking up from nightmares. I am freezing cold. My mom told me, once, that the temperature of your feet has everything to do with what your dreams are like. Maybe I'm having these awful nightmares because my feet are too cold? They stick out from under the blankets and they let in the bugs and vomit and chewing gum that sticks to my teeth. All the nightmare things.

I've been thinking about getting a dream catcher. I don't even know if that's a different band of Indians or what. I don't know a goddamned thing about Indians except that my brother and I both look darker and we used to sit on his porch and drink beer and we used to make each other laugh.

Yours,

Joey Comeau

Dear University of Victoria,

I am applying to the position for university linguistics professor with your university, because while my love is language, it is also worth noting that language's love is me, for real, and it isn't as strange as it sounds because I think you will agree that while the verb love requires an agent of a living nature, language fills that requirement nicely — living as it does in the hearts and souls of every man, woman, child, and seeing eye dog that wanders this earth with a song in masculine, feminine, or neuter's possessive pronoun's heart and mind, and I feel that working in your university program, teaching undergrads and graduate students would not be the hell that your job description evokes, but instead an opportunity to teach a love of language to a world that has decided to hate hate hate hate hate hate hate hate hate hate, and language is how we hold on to our family and how we figure out our place and how we order in a French restaurant to impress our date and hey, have you ever stopped to think that explicity is a much nicer word than explicitness on all fronts, at every border, in every way I feel this is true, and because I sat down to write them out, about a dozen times each, I feel I can speak with authority, using definiteness, definity, and seriously — it's just nicer I think, spiritually, though I'm still working on this study to try and prove it through polling of students at my current university, even though they just sort of stare at me all slack-jawed, drool making the mad dash for a pavement that couldn't help but offer more in the way of intellectual stimulation than the chasm that is the modern undergraduate mind, that

couldn't help but challenge the drool in a way that no
English composition course could hope to, not in a world
where universities are too willing to hire professors who
prescribe standard grammars as truer languages and to grant
doctorates to such nincompoops with nonsense in their
heads, no hearts in their chests, making me wonder about,
well, don't think I haven't noticed that explicity has that
little red underline in my word processor, my computer's
way of endorsing those effers and their effing prescriptions,
their nasal voices preaching "no prepositions at the ends of
sentences, unless you have to, no split infinitives, no run on
whatever, no this, no that," and I sincerely believe that
they've cheated on their significant others, and I bet they've
heard someone say something hateful toward the speech
patterns of foreigners just learning English, and laughed,
and I bet they've used the word "ebonics" knowing full well
the condescending, racist nature of the word itself, relishing
that root, "ebony," smiling at their coworkers from the
African studies department in the hall, all the while having
to consciously refrain from asking, "What is it that be the
up?" in perfect imitation of the phonetic transcripts they've
been reading about in little journals, hate rags, and maybe
they've picked up on the careful lexical selections in my
anonymous letters, in the casual threats I leave on their
answering machines, and no I can't promise that I won't
physically attack these people if you hire me, but I can
promise you this: I will be the best linguistics professor
you've ever had, the professor that students recommend to
one another, the new hotness, the rad, and in dark corners
my colleagues over in the department of "Standard English

is the one true lord" will fear the truth I bring to their students, my anger, my explicity.

Joey Comeau

Dear IBM,

Perverts are everywhere, and I'm no exception. I used to joke that I should never get a webcam. I reasoned that if I did, I would be on the Internet disgracing myself within hours. That timeline, it appears, was optimistic. A webcam came with my new keyboard, and within ten minutes of installing it, my pants were pulled down and my shirt was pulled up and I honestly couldn't choose between being mortified at myself and thinking, "If dignity means I can't do this, then fuck dignity!"

There's a weird magic to your image, though. I don't care if that sounds crazy. I've started believing in magic. Magic and ghosts and family.

I brought a Polaroid JoyCam to bed with a friend and we took photographs in the dark. It's weird to pose for yourself, your future self. How do you cater to your own tastes if your taste is the unexpected? Flash. Flash. Flash. And afterward, we sat on my bed and we looked through the pictures with the lights on, all wrapped in blankets and sweatshirts. The pictures were harshly lit and terrifying and sort of perfect in their ugliness. Our skin looked too white from the flash. We were always squinting. Our bodies didn't look natural. They looked the way nighttime photos of moles and bats always look.

We decided that we had to get rid of them. But of course we couldn't just put them in the garbage, because what if someone found them? No, we had to destroy them. I was afraid to burn them because of chemicals, so we cut them open, pushing my pocket knife between the layers and scraping away the image. I don't think that was the best idea. The chemical powder stuck to the blade. It scratched down onto my sheets.

And there's a sick feeling you get when you're scratching away your own face. We agreed we would scratch ourselves. I don't think I could have handled scratching away someone else's face. I could hardly handle mine. I woke up the next morning feeling quiet. Feeling cursed. I still have one of the photos that we missed, and I'm afraid to throw it away. I get a sick feeling in my stomach when I think about those scratched out pictures and I wish I had all of the pictures still. I would put them up on my wall, all ugly and broken and perverted and squinty-eyed and alive.

I feel weird writing this, I guess, but what if we die and nobody remembers those parts of us? What if all that's left is the censored version?

Joey Comeau

Dear General Electric,

When I was a kid, my brother and I used to sneak past the locked front doors of apartment buildings. There were four apartment buildings in my neighbourhood. One of them was harder than the others to get into, until we figured out that there was an exit in the back of the building and we could just wait out there until someone left and then catch the door. Once we were inside we just wandered the halls the same way we wandered our neighbourhood. We climbed the stairs to the very top, and there was a public balcony on this floor, just like on the others. You could stand and look out over everything.

We bought parachute men to throw from the balcony. They rocked and drifted and we took the elevator down to try and beat them to the ground, only to find them caught in bushes and trees. We bought those styrofoam planes that you have to punch out of the sheet and build, that are printed with designs on one side and are blank white on the other. They flew in spirals down to the ground, or around the side of the building. Once, my plane flew to the building across the street and down the road. It flew straight and slowly. We loved to take the elevator down and walk out the front, coming from behind the locked door, like we lived there, like we had every right.

And then, climbing the back stairs one day, we stopped to unscrew one of the light bulbs. Adrian took the next one, and then I took the next. There was a light bulb on each of

the little landings on the way up the stairs. We climbed to
the top, stealing light bulbs the whole way. We climbed
and the stairs went dark behind us, as though there was
something back there, following us up. We stole bulbs until
we were on the balcony in the sun with a shirtful each.

I want to say that we looked first, but maybe not. All I
remember for certain is that there were two kinds of bulbs.
They weren't all the same. Some were made of white glass
and some were clear. We threw bulb after bulb, as fast as we
could. There were a half dozen in the air before the
explosions started below. We never worried whether it was
safe. We lived for the danger. We lived for that crazy sound
a light bulb makes when it bursts against pavement. And
then we were running as fast as we could down the dark
concrete stairs.

I love the feeling of running down stairs. It's an activity the
body was made for, something that feels perfect and correct.

Joey Comeau

Dear Danny Carey, of Danny Carey Insurance,

I am writing to apply for the position of life insurance sales agent, and I have included my resume, which details my years of experience, as well as my years of schooling in insurance law.

But my resume doesn't explain what I have to offer the agency on a personal level. What will your customers deal with on a face-to-face basis? Well, I'm someone that they can relate to. I used to be them. I put every cent of my money into investments, into insurance. I devoted my life to planning for the future. I obsessed over what might happen. I needed contingencies. I needed plans B, C, and D.

And there's nothing wrong with that. What's good for you in the short term is often less than acceptable in the long term. Going home with the girl who has been making eyes at you across the bar is fine right now, but in two weeks you might be standing in line at the pharmacy, embarrassed.

This was how I used to think. I spent hours at the library, running risk management statistics on blow jobs. I used to grill girls on their recent sexual history, demand to see STD testing documentation. I was single for a very long time.

I devoted my time to personal forms of life insurance, to eating well, to making careful decisions, never taking risks. And while I was focusing my attention on the short term, on avoiding clear risks, it didn't occur to me that I was going to die anyway.

It didn't occur to me until a car drove through the front of my house, stopping inches from my head. A hooker stumbled out, a bomb strapped to her stomach, digital clock counting down from five minutes. Lice crawling through her hair as she threatened me with a rusty crowbar that had used needles taped to the end. She tied me down and fucked me without a condom. She wasn't going to leave until I came inside her, she said, and the clock kept counting down. Afterward, when she was climbing back into the car, I asked her if she was on the pill, and she laughed at me. She backed out onto the front lawn and exploded to death. I got a little cut on my face, from glass.

There are no contingency plans for old age. My pitch to your customers will be simple. The door will open and I will say, "You are going to die. Why are you wasting your time haggling? Pick a fucking plan and go climb a tree. Learn a new language. Write a biography of your grandmother, even if she insists that she's never done anything. Go home and tell your wife that you're tired of watching Martha Stewart every fucking night — some nights you just want to watch girls' soccer."

Joey Comeau

Dear Royal Bank,

I was thrilled to read that you are seeking temporary bilingual administrators, and I am applying for the job. I've included my resume, and I know that once you've taken a look, you will be greatly impressed. But first, let me tell you a little about myself.

I am an Acadian, with strong emotional ties to the French language, but I am not a native speaker. Since my grandfather's death, my grandmother is the only member of my family who speaks our Acadian dialect of the language. She told me that she wanted me to learn French, and I promised. I took classes, five nights a week. I threw myself into my studies for months, and after a while I found that I could hold reasonable conversations in both French and English.

I was bilingual.

By this time, I was studying toward my Master's in Business Administration, at the top of every class. When I learned of the opportunity, I decided to study abroad, finishing my MBA at a French university where I could hone my new skill. I believed that my life was starting to find its track.

On my second day in France, I was knocked to the ground. It was only a Vespa, and the doctors insisted that I wasn't seriously injured, but after the accident I started to notice gaps in my ability to speak French. The French language I had begun to love was turning back into a hodgepodge of unintelligible sounds.

It was no longer poetry in my ears. It was noise.

My sentences became simpler and simpler. My vocabulary began to narrow. And so I threw myself back into the study of the language. It was no use. If I studied the tenses, my ability to remember the vocabulary would all but vanish. If I studied vocabulary, my ability to conjugate verbs would falter.

I have never been a quitter.

There is a window of time between when I learn the language rules and when I forget them. If I study all weekend, I can function bilingually for all of Monday and well into Tuesday morning. Sometimes into Wednesday, if I spend my lunch hours reviewing. But then it is gone again.

This temporary bilingualism has made it impossible for me to find traditional bilingual work, naturally, because most jobs require the ability to speak the language all week long, not just on Mondays and Tuesdays. It has been a curse to me, but —

Actually, you know what? Fuck it. This is a stupid joke. "Temporary Bilingualism." I'm sorry. I don't know what to do anymore. I talk to my grandmother on the telephone, and I try to talk French. She's the only one left who speaks it. She never taught my father, or my aunts and uncles. She knew that you needed English to get work. When I tell her I want to learn Acadian she shakes her head. She says, "It isn't proper French. It's just a patois. You want to learn real French." But I don't. I want to learn the language of my family. I try to pick up the small differences in Acadian. *"Je sais pas"* instead of *"je ne sais pas."* It's hard. And she always switches to English.

I don't know how else to hold on.

Yours,

Joseph Comeau

Dear Farmers Dairy,

Some days I feel like all I do is sit around and calculate odds. What are the odds that this chocolate milk carton I left out overnight has drinkable chocolate milk in it?

I used to say, "Life wouldn't be as good without chocolate milk," and I sort of still believe that. But I don't know if we measure the goodness of life on some ultimate scale, or the good parts against the bad. If there was no chocolate milk, probably fruit punch would pick up the slack. Or maybe nightmares wouldn't seem so bad.

I'm teaching my grandmother to speak Arabic. Here's a language we're both terrible at. I can ask her, where is my fork? You have my fork. Do you have my fork? My name is Joey.

I am teaching her to pick locks. She's a little bewildered by all this attention, I think. I am living in the guest room. I bought some locks so we can practice. Picking locks is surprisingly easy. She learns quick, too, my grandmother. She's so sharp.

This morning she asked me, what next? I told her everything is next. We'll learn to pick pockets next, to hack computers and telephone networks, to disarm someone quickly and efficiently, to seduce anyone and steal their keycards while they sleep, to live on submarines.

We'll wake up every day and we'll tell ourselves, "Live for today, you retarded little shit. The end is near."

Joey Comeau

the end.

Joey Comeau lives in Toronto. He co-creates a comic called *A Softer World* with Emily Horne, which can be found at www.asofterworld.com. That website is also where you can find links to his other work! For instance, there is a story on there called "One Bloody Thing After Another," if you like scary stories that are also sort of sad.